Terry Tasker is James's favourite TV star. Terry knows all about pets and James wants to be just like him so he always watches Terry's pet-care show. When Pippa says she's seen Terry in person James doesn't believe her because she's always boasting. But then he comes up with a way to meet his TV hero . . . and go one up on Pippa at the same time!

Katie has something very exciting to tell all her friends . . . but so has Melanie. Katie is having a party, but it turns out that Melanie is having one too, and on the same day! They both have the same friends, so which party will everyone choose – especially their best friend Lisa? It seems that Melanie's magician will tip the balance . . . until Katie and her mum come up with some magic of their own!

These two entertaining stories appear in one volume for the first time.

# James and the TV Star

## Michael Hardcastle

**PUFFIN BOOKS**

PUFFIN BOOKS

Published by the Penguin Group
27 Wrights Lane, London W8 5TZ, England
Viking Penguin Inc., 40 West 23rd Street, New York, New York 10010, USA
Penguin Books Australia Ltd, Ringwood, Victoria, Australia
Penguin Books Canada Ltd, 2801 John Street, Markham, Ontario, Canada L3R 1B4
Penguin Books (NZ) Ltd, 182–190 Wairau Road, Auckland 10, New Zealand

Penguin Books Ltd, Registered Offices: Harmondsworth, Middlesex, England

*James and the TV Star* first published in Blackie Bears by Blackie and Son Limited 1986;
*The Magic Party* first published in Blackie Bears by Blackie and Son Limited 1988
Published in one volume in Puffin Books 1990
1 3 5 7 9 10 8 6 4 2

Printed and bound in Great Britain by
Cox & Wyman Ltd, Reading

# CONTENTS

# James and the TV Star

Illustrated by Pat MacCarthy

James was fed up with Pippa, the girl next door. She was always boasting. Every day she boasted she had seen something new. She had seen a circus, she had seen the stars through a telescope, she had seen a rabbit hanging up in a shop. She was a Know-All.

'I've seen inside a real

ambulance,' she told James.
'The back doors were open, so I
had a really good look. The
blankets were red.'

'I know a boy who went in an
ambulance once. He fell and hurt
his head and they had to take
him to hospital,' James replied.

'That's not as good as actually
seeing inside an ambulance for
yourself,' Pippa said.

James knew that. For a
moment he wished an ambulance
would come and take Pippa
away, except then she would be
able to boast that she'd been in
hospital!

James and Pippa went to the
same school. Pippa was a year

older than James but they were
always meeting because their
mothers were friends. Their
mothers would stand and talk

for ages. So James often had to
listen to Pippa's boasting.

James had a new, very smart
red-and-green sweater. It was a
very special sweater and he
planned to wear it as often as he

could. Of course, Know-All
Pippa had something to say
about it as soon as she saw it.
But, for once, she said the right
thing.

'I saw Terry Tasker wearing a
red-and-green sweater just like
that yesterday,' she said in her
usual boasting voice.

'Terry Tasker wasn't *on* TV
yesterday,' James shot back at
her with glee.

He knew what he was talking
about. Terry Tasker was his
favourite person on TV and
James never missed his show. He
was the man who knew
everything about animals. All
animals, all shapes, all sizes, all

colours. Terry knew how to look
after them, what to give them to
eat and how to make them better
if they were poorly. What's more,
Terry actually went to visit the
animals where they lived. That
was better for them than taking
them to the TV studio. His
programme was called "Terry
Tasker's Tips". James loved it.
He wanted to be just like Terry
when he grew up. He wanted to
do Terry's job. Already he had
started to act like Terry and
dress like him, when he had the
chance. Terry Tasker had
a red-and-green sweater he
often wore on TV. James had
made his mum knit him a

sweater just like it. There was really nothing Pippa could tell James about Terry Tasker.

'I didn't say I'd seen him on TV yesterday,' Pippa pointed out smugly. 'I saw him in person.'

James was puzzled by that. 'You're joking with me, aren't you?' he said.

'Course not!' said Pippa. 'I'm just telling you exactly what I saw.'

James still didn't believe her. He walked away a couple of steps, then changed his mind and turned back. If she was telling the truth, then he wanted to know more. Pippa was still leaning on the gate with her

chin resting on her hands. She'd been watching him.

'Go on then, Pippa, tell me *where* you saw Terry Tasker!' he said.

'I saw Mr Smarty-Sweater Terry Tasker at Holly Tree Hall,' said Pippa. 'My best friend Debbie lives at the cottage by the entrance to the Hall. Her house is called Holly Tree Cottage. I've seen inside the Hall, of course. It's very—sinister.'

James didn't know what sinister meant. He simply pretended he did. He thought about Terry Tasker at Holly Tree Hall. Could Pippa be telling the truth after all?

'What was Terry doing there?' he asked.

'He was looking at a sick tortoise,' Pippa replied. 'Trying to make it better. He's coming back on Friday to see if it is better. He told everybody he hoped the tortoise would be as perky as a pixie by then. But I don't think it will be. It looked pretty dopey to me.'

'Terry Tasker will make it better,' James said confidently. 'He makes everyone better. He is fan-tas-tic! Terry is perfect.'

Perfect was James's favourite word. Pippa, he thought, was the opposite of perfect. So he was glad when she said she had to go now. James wandered off to his garden to see his own tortoise.

He was called Topper and he was very, very, very old. But Topper always seemed healthy. James believed that was because he fed him on cooked French beans. Though it might take him a week to finish a meal, Topper never left a scrap of French bean.

Now James found Topper having a rest under the plum tree.

James picked up a bean from Topper's own dish and offered him a nibble. He held the bean by the tips of finger and thumb,

just as Terry Tasker did when
he fed animals. Topper opened
his eyes and took the bean.

'Perfect, Topper, perfect,' said
James, scratching Topper's long

neck. 'Terry Tasker would think you were perfect if ever he met you.'

It was James's greatest wish to meet and talk to Terry Tasker. Now his chance had come! He made up his mind then and there that he would go to Holly Tree Hall to say hello to his hero. But how was he going to get there? His Mum was going to see Auntie Sarah in hospital at lunchtime on Friday, so she wouldn't be able to take him. His Dad would be at work and James couldn't think of anyone else who might help. But he knew that he would have to think of something. He couldn't miss this

chance of meeting Terry.

'You're very quiet, James,' his mum said several times that evening.

'I'm thinking,' he replied.

'That makes a change,' she said with a smile.

'What does sinister mean, Mum?' he asked.

'A bit strange and scary,' she told him. 'Why?'

'Oh, nothing,' said James. He felt a bit worried. He knew he'd have to be brave: brave to go to a sinister house and brave to go there on his own. Still, he would

do anything to meet Terry Tasker.

The next day was Thursday. Pippa cornered James at playtime. She had some news for him.

'We've got a lobster at home,' she told him. 'My dad caught it at the seaside last night. It's huge. We're going to eat it tomorrow night.'

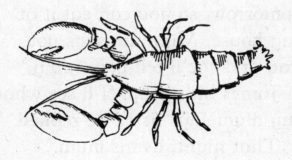

'I've seen a lobster,' James replied. 'It's nothing special.'

'This one is because it's ALIVE!' Pippa went on. 'I bet you've never seen a living lobster, have you?'

James agreed he hadn't. But he didn't want to see a lobster that Pippa was going to eat.

'Well, you're going to see it,' Pippa said gleefully. 'I know you're having a packed lunch tomorrow, so you can eat it at my house. My mum says you can and she'll tell your mum.'

James bit his lip. 'I'll see what my mum says first,' he replied.

That night, as his mum tucked him up in bed, James

told her, 'Pippa says I've got to
have my packed lunch at her
house tomorrow.'

'You don't *have* to, James.
Pippa doesn't decide what we

do. You can go to Pippa's or eat your lunch at school. I really don't mind. It's up to you.'

'I'll think about it,' said James with a yawn.

After his mum had left his bedroom James stared up at the big poster on his wall. The

poster gave a list of Terry
Tasker's Top Ten Tips and had
a colour picture of his hero.

'I've got a perfect plan to see
you in person tomorrow, Terry,'
James told the poster before he
fell asleep.

On Friday morning James got
up and put on his red-and-green
sweater. His mum gave him his
favourite food for his packed
lunch. Sausage sandwiches and
crisps and marmalade cake.
While his mum wasn't looking,
James peeped inside the fridge.
He wanted to take something for
Terry, something that would be
really good. Wrapping it in a
see-through bag, he put it in his

box with his packed lunch.

'Have a nice time if you go to Pippa's,' his mum said as she saw him off at the door.

'I hope Auntie Sarah is feeling better,' James remembered to tell his mum.

At school James kept out of

Pippa's way at playtime by playing football with Shiva, his best friend, and some other boys. Then, at lunchtime, he simply told her: 'I'm not coming to your house. My mum said I could please myself, so I am doing.' Pippa was very cross but she couldn't make him change his mind. So she had to go home alone.

When he was sure no one was looking, James slipped out of the playground. He made his way down the avenue to the bus stop. The local bus went straight through to Holly Tree Hall. So all he had to do was catch it. While he waited for the blue-

and-white bus he sat on the long
seat, swung his legs and scoffed
his sausage sandwiches and
marmalade cake. The crisps he
would save until later. It felt
lovely to eat his lunch all by
himself in the open air. He
finished it just as the bus rolled
up.

'That's perfect,' he told
himself.

James paid his fare out of his pocket money. Luckily the bus driver didn't ask him why he was on his own. So he sat back to enjoy the ride and nibble at his crisps. But then he started thinking about the sinister house. Would it be dark and spooky? Would fierce animals be roaming about? Would it be haunted?

Would he be able to get in? He began to worry again.

When he got there, Holly Tree Hall didn't look sinister at all. It seemed to be made of wood. It was painted all in black-and-white. To James it looked a cheerful place in the sunshine. Then he spotted Terry Tasker himself on the big lawn, and it all became perfect. Terry was wearing his red-and-green sweater. James looked down at his own red-and-green sweater and smiled to himself.

Terry was kneeling in the centre of a small group of people. One man held a TV camera, another had a long

microphone. They were all looking at a tortoise. Terry was shaking his head slowly in a very sad way. James knew his hero needed cheering up.

Everyone was so busy with the tortoise that no one saw James arrive. He took his gift from his lunch box and hurried over to Terry on the lawn.

'Hello, Terry,' he said. 'My name is James and I've brought a present for you and the sick

tortoise.' He held up the see-through bag. 'It's cooked French beans. My tortoise, Topper, loves cooked French beans and I thought this tortoise might, too.'

Terry looked startled for a moment. Then he smiled his famous TV smile at James.

'What a great idea,' he said. 'Speedie here hasn't been eating much. He doesn't seem keen on anything I've offered him. Perhaps he needs something really special to revive his appetite. So let's try him on your magic beans, James. Here goes.'

Everyone watched keenly as Terry emptied the bag of beans on the grass. Then he held out

one long bean between the tips
of finger and thumb. Nothing
happened for a few moments.
The tortoise really did look
rather dopey. But, suddenly, he
began to perk up. He opened his
eyes wide and his nose lifted. He
began to nibble the bean. Soon
he took another—and then
another.

'Hey, your trick has worked like a dream!' said Terry, his smile growing wider than ever. 'Well done, James. I think you've saved Speedie's life—and my show. Your tip is definitely tops.'

'That's just great, Terry,' said the cameraman. 'I kept the camera rolling from the moment James came on. Didn't miss a thing. It'll be a great sequence.'

'What's a sequence?' asked James.

'A sequence is any piece of film, any story if you like, that we use on the show,' replied Terry. He fondly rubbed the back of Speedie's head. Speedie was still gobbling up French

beans. 'So the sequence of you and me and Speedie will be in the next programme. You'll be able to see yourself saving Speedie's life. Everyone will see Speedie looking as perky as a pixie. Perfect!'

James grinned. He was going to be on TV! Better still, he was going to be on TV with Terry Tasker—his hero!

He'd make sure to tell everyone when the show was going to be on, especially Pippa. She would see *him* on TV. Afterwards she'd go round telling everyone she had seen James on TV with Terry Tasker!

That would be perfect, too.

# The Magic Party

Illustrated by
Vanessa Julian-Ottie

'Listen Lisa,' said Katie
eagerly, 'I've got something
terrific to tell you. To tell
everybody.'

'Tell me first,' said Lisa. 'After
all, I am your best friend.'

But Katie wanted to tell
everyone at once. She led the
way across the playground to

the corner by the old bakery
where all secrets were swapped.

'Jessica—Sharmilla—Bobby!
Come over here, quick!' she
called loudly. 'I've something
very special to tell you all.'

Then she spotted Melanie,
who seemed to be heading for
the same part of the playground.
'Mel! Come and listen to this.'

Melanie just waved a hand to
show she'd heard. She was
holding a package in her other
hand and chattering away to
Ross and Belinda. Just behind
them was Simon, trying to catch
everything that was said. Simon
hated to miss out on anything.

'Oh, come on, Katie, don't

keep us waiting!' Jessica
pleaded, putting her hands
together as if she were praying.
'I hate having to wait for
anything.'

'You'll know in a moment,
Jess,' Katie promised with a
smile.

'Is it to do with school, what you're going to tell us, Katie?' Sharmilla wanted to know.

'Nothing at all to do with school,' Katie said firmly. With one hand she was dipping into her new shoulder bag, her fingers tightening round a bundle of envelopes.

She grinned at Lisa, who pulled one of her very funny faces. Then Lisa popped her fingers in and out of her ears to show it was time for the secret to be let out.

The two groups arrived at the same place at exactly the same moment. So between them they formed a large huddle. Vikki,

noticing what was going on,
raced towards them.

'Wait for me, wait for me!' she
yelled. 'Don't do anything till I
get there!'

Katie and Melanie waited
until she joined them. With a
quick look round, Vikki placed
herself midway between Katie
and Melanie.

'Go on, then,' she urged, folding her arms across her chest and rocking her head from side to side. 'I can see you've both got something special to say. So who's going first?'

'You can!' said Katie and Melanie in the same instant, each looking at the other and being very polite. It was such a surprise they'd both said exactly the same thing that everyone laughed.

'Oh well, me first then,' said Melanie with a smile. She quickly sorted through the pile of envelopes in her hand and gave one to Katie. 'Here you are, Katie, you get the first one.

It's an invitation to my birthday
party the Sunday after next. I
want everyone to be there. It's
going to be very, very special.'

Katie stared. She couldn't
believe what was happening.

'But, but...' She began again.
'But, Melanie, it's MY birthday
party the Sunday after next.
I've got an invitation here for
you—and, well, everyone.'

'Oh no!' groaned Lisa. 'Not on the same day!'

'Hey, that's no good!' Simon said, looking very upset. 'If they're at the same time we'll have to miss out on one of them. I'd hate that!'

'Are they at the same time, Katie?' Jessica asked.

'Mine's in the afternoon,' Katie said, and glanced at Melanie. 'Is yours?'

Melanie just nodded.

'Well, you can change the day—one of you,' Vikki pointed out. 'Then everything will be fine. We can all go to two parties. Terrific!'

'I'd like that!' said Simon.

'Is Sunday your actual birthday, Katie?' Melanie wanted to know.

'Well, no, it's Saturday. But we have to go to London for my cousin's birthday on the Saturday. It's our turn to go there this year, Mum says. That's why we're having my party the next day. And Mum's getting some videos in London specially for my party.'

Melanie looked pleased with herself. 'We're having a real magician!' she said proudly. 'He's called Marvo the Magician. It's going to be a magic party.'

'Oh, that's terrific!' Vikki exclaimed.

'Wow!' said Simon, opening his eyes as wide as his mouth.

'Fantastic!' said Belinda.

'I've always wanted to see a real magician!' said Lisa.

'So have I,' said Vikki.

Katie said nothing, nothing at all. Her heart sank. I'd have liked to have a real magician at my party, too, she thought, but she knew that was impossible. All Mum's money seemed to go on their old car, the Moving Museum. Still, Mum was a brilliant cook, so the food would be special. And she was always full of ideas, so she'd be able to invent some good games. And then they'd have the videos.

My party will be magic in a different way, Katie told herself. She gave out her party

63

invitations to everyone: and everyone looked pleased to get one. 'I'd like to come to both parties,' Simon announced.

'You're just greedy,' laughed Jessica.

Katie wondered which of her friends would come to her party. She particularly wanted Lisa to be there.

'You will come to my party, won't you?' she asked Lisa on their way back into school.

Lisa glanced across at Melanie. 'I don't know yet for sure, Katie,' she replied. 'Are you going to have a magician, too?'

'Maybe,' Katie said vaguely.

'Or maybe something even better.' Then, before Lisa could ask her any more questions, she ran inside.

After school Katie rushed straight home. Her mum was working on the car, which was parked outside the shed at the end of the lane. She was looking a bit fed up.

'Something wrong with the petrol pump,' she explained, jabbing at the engine. 'That's the trouble with old cars, there's always something to put right. Still, I'll get there in the end. Had a good day, darling?'

'Not really,' Katie replied, crossing her arms under her chin and looking very glum. Then she told her mum about the party problems. 'What can we do, Mum?'

'Well, there's one thing we could do, Katie,' her mum said. 'We could simply have your party on another day—perhaps the following week. Then—'

'Oh no!' Katie wailed. 'I'd

hate that! I mean, I wanted it
on my proper birthday, on the
Saturday. But I had to change
it because of going to London.
So I want the party as near as
possible to the real day. I don't
think birthdays should be moved
about like, like the hands of a
clock!'

Her mum laughed. 'Well, I

agree with you really,' she said. 'I just thought a change of date would give you a chance to go to Melanie's party.'

'I expect Melanie's will be good,' Katie admitted. 'But mine will be better.'

'You know what you are, don't you?' her mum said.

'What?' said Katie.

'You're stubborn, that's what!' said her mum. 'That's how you get your own way.'

Katie laughed. 'Could you make us some of that spooky food, Mum?' she asked. 'Cobweb squash and broomstick-burgers and those witch biscuits with red and green eyes? They're terrific!'

'Maybe,' said her mum. 'And
we'll need something really
special for the games. Actually,
I was talking to Mrs Cheng
down the lane today and she's
given me rather a bright idea.
Listen...'

At school next day Katie asked Lisa if she was coming to her party.

'Well...' Lisa began.

'You'll be missing something really good if you don't come,' Katie told her.

Lisa rolled her eyes, one of her favourite tricks. 'Such as?' she wanted to know.

'Well, listen to this: we're going to have a dragon at my party! A real, moving dragon with fire shooting out of its mouth! How about that?'

For once Lisa didn't make one of her funny faces. She just looked amazed.

'Will it really breathe out fire

that can, well, scorch you?' she
asked.

'Of course. That's what proper
dragons do, isn't it?' Katie
replied.

'Why are you having a dragon
at your party?' asked Vikki, who
had just joined them and heard
what Katie said.

'Because this year the Chinese New Year falls on my party day, that's why. And Chinese dragons always turn up at parties to celebrate the New Year. That's what Mrs Cheng says. And she's Chinese, so she should know. So that's how we're getting one. A proper Chinese dragon.'

'This I've got to see!' Lisa exclaimed.

'Me, too,' said Vikki.

'And me!' Simon chimed in. He had heard Lisa's excited voice and he, Jessica, Ross, Belinda and Sharmilla had all come to listen.

Katie was delighted. Mum's

great idea was working.
Everyone wanted to be at her
party.

'Well, you'll all have to wear
something red,' she told them.
'That's very important.'

Lisa looked puzzled. 'Why,
Katie?' she asked.

'Because that's the magic

colour for dragons,' said Katie. 'Didn't you know? The Chinese think red's a very lucky colour.'

'Will a red headband do?' Jessica asked.

'Well, if you like,' said Katie. 'But red tights will be better. People might not be able to see the headband.'

That puzzled everyone. 'Why?' they all wanted to know.

Katie grinned. 'You'll find out at the party. But you'll have to wait till then.'

'I wish your party was tomorrow, Katie,' Ross said with a sigh. 'I can't wait for it to begin. It'll be magic with a dragon.'

A few days later, at going home time, Melanie came to talk to Katie in the cloakroom.

'You know, Katie, you could still come to my party if you wanted to,' she said. 'I wish you would. You could easily just change the date of your party. Then I could come as well.'

'It can't be changed, Mel,'
Katie replied. 'It's the Chinese
New Year's Day. We're going to
have some very special games.
And the dragon's coming, of
course. Why don't you change
the date of your party? Then
you could come to mine.'

Melanie shook her head and
her long blonde hair danced.
'Marvo the Magician has been
booked for ages. He's very
popular, you know. He wouldn't
be free on another day for—for
months.'

'Oh well, I hope you have a
great time,' Katie said
cheerfully. 'I'm sure you will.'

'How many are going to your

76

party, Katie?' Melanie asked.

'Don't know exactly. But lots and lots, I think.'

'I thought so,' Melanie said.

'Hey, look at that!' Ross said excitedly to Belinda as they arrived at Katie's for the party. 'Look at that dragon's head on the door!'

'Shows we're at the right house,' Belinda said. 'I think this is going to be really good.'

It was such a cold winter's day that everyone was given a hot drink as they came in: a steaming mug of red fruit juice. 'It's what dragons drink to set their breath on fire!' Katie explained.

'Where's the real dragon, Katie?' Lisa wanted to know.

'He'll be here in a little while,' said Katie's mum. 'But first you've all got to look for him. I'd start in the old laundry room if I were you...'

Lisa was the first to get there because she knew Katie's house

so well. And there, lying on the washing machine, was a long green tail.

'Who made that?' Sharmilla wanted to know. 'It looks just like the real thing with those bubbly bits.'

'I helped Mum,' Katie said. 'She used some old felt.'

'It's got a message on,'
Belinda said. She read aloud:

> 'To find the very next bit of me,
> Look closely where we keep the tea.

'What does that mean?' asked
Ross.

'It's a clue in a treasure hunt,'
explained Vikki. She had won a
treasure hunt at another party.
'Where do you keep the tea,
Katie?'

'You'll have to work that out,'
Katie said.

'Must be the kitchen!' Ross
said and so everyone rushed
there. But it turned out to be the
pantry and it was Sharmilla
who found the next part of the

dragon on a shelf near the
teabags.

'Hey, you can fit it over your
head,' Sharmilla said, lifting the
green-painted hollow box to
show everyone. 'And the tail fits
this end. Oh, and there's another
message...'

They had a hectic time hunting the missing pieces of the dragon's body all over the house and then fitting them together. The clues led them to the bathroom, the dining-room, then up to the attic and down to the cellar. At last the only part of the red-and-green-and-gold dragon left to find was its head.

Ross read out the final clue:

'If you look out of Katie's window,
What you'll see is a dazzling glow.'

They all rushed upstairs to Katie's bedroom and crowded round the window, staring into the gloomy winter afternoon. Suddenly, a sparkler flared up—

then another—and yet another.

'Look!' Lisa yelled. 'A
dragon's head, all lit up in the
dark. Coming down the path on
its own! That's magic!'

They all crowded closer,
trying to get a better view.

'Look at the red fire in its
mouth!' cried Ross.

It was a dazzling mask. Katie and her mum had painted it with luminous paint so that it glowed in the dark. Katie's mum was dressed in black, so no one could see her walking down the path, holding the mask up high.

She called to them: 'Come on down and change into a dragon!'

'Can we really all get into it?' Belinda asked when they were all in the sitting-room.

Katie's mum was busily making sure the body parts were all joined together.

'That's the idea,' she said. 'It's made so you can hold it on your shoulders. Only your legs will

show underneath. That's why
we wanted you to wear red
tights or red socks. This is the
amazing red-legged dragon!'

Katie and Lisa shared the big mask that was the head. They could each see out through an eye-hole. Lisa kept popping her tongue out through the mouth. Their friends lined up to make the body. The tail bounced along behind them.

'It's just like dressing up—only better,' Simon said.

'Come on, keep following me!' Katie called.

'Where are we going?' Ross asked. He was at the end.

'Visiting,' said Katie. 'First we're going to call on the Chinese family down the lane and wish them luck for the New Year. That's what dragons do

on New Year's Day in China.'
'Oh, great!' said Sharmilla.
'We're going outside, just like a
real parade. Everybody'll see us.'
Light snow was falling as the
Great Red-Legged Dragon
made its way slowly down the
lane. Katie's mum kept setting

off fire-crackers. People out for
a Sunday walk cheered and
clapped when they met the
amazing glowing dragon.

'We turn right here!' Katie
yelled. And the red-legged
dragon turned, a little
awkwardly, into a wide
gateway. Standing at the door
were Mr and Mrs Cheng,
clapping for joy. Mrs Cheng
was wearing a red dress and her
husband had on a red tie.

'Oh, thank you, thank you
for coming,' they greeted the
dragon. 'This is the best dragon
visit we have ever had.'

'Happy New Year!' called out
Katie and Lisa and their
friends.

Mr Cheng handed an
envelope to each of his visitors.

'It contains a present for you,'

he explained. 'It is a little money. One of our Chinese customs, you see. Happy New Year! Happy birthday, Katie!'

The dragon bowed and backed out of the gateway.

'Now where to?' asked Ross, when they were all in the lane.

'Wait and see,' said Katie mysteriously. She led the dragon round the corner and down the road. 'Stop!' she said.

They were outside Melanie's house.

Katie and Lisa peered through the eye-holes in the dragon's head. They could see Melanie and her friends in the front room, laughing at someone in a strange and marvellous costume. 'That must be Marvo the Magician,' whispered Lisa.

The dragon made its way up the path and Katie rang the doorbell. Melanie opened the door, looking very surprised.

'Happy Chinese New Year!'

Katie cried. 'Happy birthday, Melanie.' She and Lisa took off the dragon mask.

'Katie! Lisa! What a lovely surprise,' said Melanie. 'Come in, all of you, and meet Marvo the Magician.'

'Two parties in one day!' exclaimed Simon, who could hardly believe his luck.

'Two magic parties, you mean,' said Lisa and everyone laughed.